For my beautiful and brilliant firstborn, August.

Always believe.

—N.R.

Especially for Leon and Rashad

—C.P.B.

Text copyright © 2021 by Nancy Redd
Jacket art and interior illustrations copyright © 2021 by Charnelle Pinkney Barlow

All rights reserved. Published in the United States by Random House Children's Books,
a division of Penguin Random House LLC, New York.

Random House and the colophon are registered trademarks of Penguin Random House LLC.

Visit us on the Web! rhcbooks.com

Educators and librarians, for a variety of teaching tools, visit us at RHTeachersLibrarians.com

Library of Congress Cataloging-in-Publication Data is available upon request.
ISBN 978-0-593-17814-0 (trade) — ISBN 978-0-593-17815-7 (lib. bdg.) — ISBN 978-0-593-17816-4 (ebook)

The artist used watercolor, gouache, colored pencil, pastels, and digital accents to create the illustrations for this book.
The text of this book is set in 15-point Filson Pro.
Interior design by Elizabeth Tardiff

MANUFACTURED IN CHINA
10 9 8 7 6 5 4 3 2 1
First Edition

The Real Santa

By

Nancy Redd

Illustrated by

Charnelle Pinkney Barlow

Random House New York

I love, love, love Santa. His happy face is all over our home— sitting on our Christmas tree, smiling on our gift wrap, and stitched on to my sweater.

Santa's on our front door, on our mailbox . . . even on Grandma and Grandpa's car! Every Christmas Eve, my grandparents drive to our house and spend the night with us. It's one of our family traditions.

After dinner, Grandpa hands me a present. Grandma tells me to open it carefully with my little sister. I help her untie the bow, and we both look inside the box.

First, we see a cherry-red hat. Then a bushy beard appears. Next, we find a pair of twinkling brown eyes and a jiggly belly, and we know who it is. . . .

Santa!

He's holding a long scroll filled with names. I check to make sure my sister and I are on Santa's list. . . . We are!

"Ho, ho, ho!" Daddy says as he carries a tray of mugs from the kitchen. "Who wants cocoa?"

I take a big sip and feel something sticky on my top lip.

"Look at my mustache!" I say.

Mommy laughs and takes a picture. "You look just like a mini Santa."
I don't want our new Santa to get spilled on, so I put down my cocoa and
stand him on the fireplace, right in the middle of our Santa collection.

We have so many Santas in our home, and none of them look the same. Some have thick beards and bellies. Some wear bright red suits and black boots. Many ride in sleighs and carry big sacks of toys. One of my favorite Santas rides on a surfboard, catching a wave!

I love all my Santas, but on Christmas Eve, only one matters—the *real* Santa. Which one could he be?

Maybe Daddy knows. He's setting out a plate of Christmas cookies.
"Daddy, which one of our Santas looks like the *real* Santa?"

"I don't know, little man," he says. "Maybe Mommy knows?"

"I don't think Santa wants us to know what he looks like," Mommy says, carrying carrots for the reindeer. "That's why he comes so late at night."

"No one has ever seen the real Santa, sweetie," Grandma says. She's pouring a big glass of milk for Santa.

No one?

"Grandpa, what about you?"

"Nope," says Grandpa as he braids my sister's hair for bed. "Your mama wanted to take his picture once, when she was your age, but she couldn't stay awake."

This gives me a great big idea.

I ask Mommy if I can borrow her camera. She smiles, hands me a gift bag from under the tree, and says, "Happy early Christmas." I can't believe my luck. *Thank you, Mommy!*

At bedtime, we all read a story together and say good night.

As soon as my sister falls asleep, I tiptoe back downstairs.

All night long, I camp out under the Christmas tree with my camera.
I am determined to stay awake and catch the real Santa in action!
I sing Christmas carols.
I count ornaments.

But Santa takes too long to come. . . .

Dozens of Santas
dance around my dreams.

Which one could the real Santa be?
Does he wear a red or golden hat?
Is his beard gray or black?
Are the toys in a satchel,
or does he carry a sack?

In my sleep, I hear footsteps at the fireplace
and presents sliding under the tree.

Santa!

I try opening my eyes to see him, but I'm so tired that everything looks blurry.

Then I feel myself being picked up and carried to bed. I sneak a quick peek, and that's all I need.

Santa looks just like I hoped he would—

Santa looks just like me.